T0127407

PAUSE FOR BREATH

ALSO BY ROBYN SARAH

LITERARY CRITICISM

Little Eurekas: A Decade's Thoughts on Poetry (2007)

POETRY

A Day's Grace (2003)

Questions About The Stars (1998)

The Touchstone: Poems New and Selected (1992)

Becoming Light (1987)

Anyone Skating On That Middle Ground (1984)

Three Sestinas (1984)

The Space Between Sleep and Waking (1981)

Shadowplay (1978)

SHORT STORIES

Promise of Shelter (1997)

A Nice Gazebo (1992)

PAUSE FOR BREATH

ROBYN SARAH

PAUSE FOR BREATH

POEMS

BIBLIOASIS

FIRST EDITION

Library and Archives Canada Cataloguing in Publication

Sarah, Robyn, 1949-
    Pause for breath / Robyn Sarah.

Poems.
ISBN 978-1-897231-59-3

    I. Title.

PS8587.A3765P28 2009   C811'.54   C2009-904583-4

Readied for the press by Eric Ormsby.

Cover Image: D. R. Cowles, *Oranges with Bowl (Musée
archéologique, Rabat, Morocco)*

Canada Council Conseil des Arts
for the Arts   du Canada

Canadian Patrimoine
Heritage   canadien

ONTARIO ARTS COUNCIL
CONSEIL DES ARTS DE L'ONTARIO

We gratefully acknowledge the support of the Canada Council
for the Arts, Canadian Heritage, and the Ontario Arts Council
for our publishing program.

PRINTED AND BOUND IN CANADA

For L. and N.,
who go on surprising me,
and who keep me open.

PAUSE FOR BREATH

I. A Place of Ruin

II. Heat of the Immediate

III. The Briefest Room

I. A Place of Ruin

In the Middle of the Night

Something fell.
Where?
It seemed to be in the house.
Downstairs?
I heard –
I thought I heard something fall.

Did something fall?
What fell?
I thought I heard –
Was there a noise downstairs?
Did I dream it?
What did you hear?

Downstairs.
It sounded like something falling.
In the house, do you think?
It seemed –
I thought –
Could it have been outside?

Outside or in the house.
But where in the house – ?
Something left out of place,
or put away carelessly?
Knocked over, somehow – ?
By the wind – ?

– Waiting for the other
shoe to drop. (Hearts *sink*.
Hopes *plummet*.) Something fell:
was it our face?
the towers?
an empire?

Wake

The game is worth the candle, or it's not.
But what's more worth the candle than the game?
The time to strike is when the iron's hot.

Beneath the floor, the creeping spread of rot.
Soft in the middle now our souls, for shame.
The game is worth the candle, or it's not.

Once was a dream. Ground Zero marks the spot
It tumbled. Was the weakness in the frame?
The time to strike is when the iron's hot.

Once was a dream: how soon the sons forgot
To prize its estimate, except in name!
The game is worth the candle, or it's not.

Snatched molten from the fire, the melting-pot:
Crucible of our virtue and our blame.
The time to strike is when the iron's hot –

In grief still raw, with wisdom dearly bought,
To forge anew a hand to hold the flame.
The game is worth the candle, or it's not.
The time to strike is when the iron's hot.

A.D. 2007

A tyrant is hanged on the eve
of a New Year. No fanfare.
People are feeling quiet.
On the bus, some of the young
in whose hands the future lies
are overheard: *So, asshole,
was Santa good ta ya?*

At home it has come down
to a year of cleanup
and weeding, of making room.
Digging out from under our own
lives let slide.
Corrupted information is
stinking in cyberspace.
The days are spookily warm.
In the corner of every eye
is that madman building a bomb.

We would have to backtrack
through so much claptrap
to get to where things took a
wrong turn. And wouldn't it be
too late? Where, anyway,
do we think we're going?
Where are we going?
Nowhere very fast.

Underneath it all:
the wish to begin again
like a bankrupt, with nothing
but a clean slate.

The Star

Back then there were things
you could get free with two box tops,
cereal box promises, *Hey Kids!*
Collect the Whole Set!
while in your bowl the golden puffs
of rice or rye snap-crackled their way
to milksop sogginess.
(Tin whistles. Flying saucers. Molded
plastic dinosaurs, with corrugated spines
you could gnaw while doing homework.
And always that chance to nail
a bigger prize – the 3-speed bike,
the trip to Disneyland – if you were
one of the lucky winners . . .)
It was a tinsel world
of innocence – Mom
in a frilled apron, the dog
winsome, grinning in the kitchen
on a black and white chequer
of vinyl tile, waxed see-your-face clean:
beginning of an age
of greed and heedlessness.

Still, it was an age
of homely miracles: tissues
that popped up one at a time,
instant pudding, see-through plastic wrap,
crystals of beverage (*Just Add Water!*),
Power Crystals in powdered laundry soap.
Things went better with Coke.
And in the living room, newly enshrined,
the greatest homely miracle of all –

the cabinet of glowing picture tubes
that showed you these, and
weekly shenanigans of shadow-friends
brought to you by the lot.

And what has changed? So little
and so much. It's all in colour now,
and every ante has been upped
past every paradigm of decency,
and it has grown and spread
around the world, to dirt-floored hovels
in hill villages, sowing desire
in scab-faced children for baubles
and blue jeans.
                            – But it began
a tinsel world of innocence.
The black and white TV.
Remember how it flashed
and flickered when you turned the knob
to OFF? And how the crackling screen
went dark around an incandescent star
that slowly shrank
till just a pinpoint of white light
still lingered, ticking, in the gloom . . .

and then went out?

Screens

Privately, we have
other thoughts. Not the ones
we broadcast or endorse
across the garden fence.
We hold our tongues
to keep the peace.
Silence implies consent.
To all appearances we
seem content.

What if the kingmakers
hoist dimwits on their shoulders,
and the people make loud noise?
What if they crown another crook,
bedeck a charlatan with laurel wreaths
and hail false prophets?
When was it ever otherwise?
The dance of money
is the only dance,
and nothing draws crowds
like a crowd.

Let's not be tedious,
and let's not multiply
the smoke of words.
Let's not undress the emperor.
Not while the smell of scorched meat
wafts from the restaurants
into the street,

and the latest model cars
gleam in the showrooms.
The glass has a cool stem.
Fill it again.
The say of the day
is an empty chant in mouths.

Green, green, green, green, green.
It doesn't mean a thing.

Breakfast and Morning Paper

Trouble has come to our
neighbour's house.

Is it human to hope
in the face of bad odds?

If indeed the tide has turned,
then it is right now bearing our way

a raft of havoc-wreaking storms,
earthquakes, mutated viruses and car bombs.

Are we marching unto war?
Is it the death-knell of the West we hear?

— We don't, it seems, really think so.
Our crisp new agendas say no.

We have things booked right into June,
it's one of our tricks.

The porridge is gummy, and sticks
to the serving spoon.

A Prayer for Prayer

God! I am dead empty.
Pour me full again.
I am leaden; lighten me.
My cables are cut.

Pour me full again,
a freshly brimming cup.
My cables are cut.
Oh, hook me up!

A freshly brimming cup,
sunstruck, flashing sun's fire:
oh, hook me up,
string me like a lyre

sunstruck, flashing sun's fire,
by this wintry window.
String me like a lyre
and let the hours pluck,

by this wintry window,
a tune from taut gut.
Oh, let the hours pluck
a psalm: forsake me not!

A tune from taut gut:
I am leaden; lighten me.
A psalm: *Forsake me not,*
God! I am dead empty.

Dry Spring

No words, no will to words.
April days are bright.
My hope's in hiding.

A whistling among the bare twigs.
Nothing wants to ignite.

Drawing my sadness over me
like a thin blanket, what
shall I fasten on? or let me unhook.

Wind chasing sand along the curb?
Blind sparrow chirp?

April days are bright.
I do not like what life has scribbled
in my blank book.

Song

Think, a hundred years from now
what will remain of this day's grief?
What, of this mother
and her mad daughter,
and all the wild rains that were?
O all the tears,
the ones she cried, and those
that cried themselves, flushed
from her eyes without her?
Unruly rivulets!
Such storms of water!

Of this day's grief, what will remain?
Only a song.
Only this song – sprung
like those rivers wrung
unbidden out of the rock
of hopeless hope,
the diehard hope
that will not drown in tears
but lives for years,
a mother's hope
to dash herself upon.

How briefly wild wings beat
against rude weather!
What will remain?
What – of this daughter
and her sad mother,
after they're gone?
Only a song.

And who will sing along?

Pent

I threw the say
of how I felt
out from me

like a pebble
into the stream:
ripples, then none,

the small tight stone
in my chest, there
no longer (but deep

within, another
already forming
where it had been –

As a storm-lopped tree

As a storm-lopped tree corrects its shape
over a few green seasons, so time
closes around the hole in itself
left by the terrible event.

(in the quiet room suddenly the ice
in your glass hisses and cracks –)

So years have carried you, far beyond
the site of your old derailment,
the place where once you caused
harm to yourself and others;
it is behind you now,
and the damage, behind us all.

The chain belt of time
runs around and around.
Moon walks where it wants to,
like cats in high places.
Sun gilds the buildings . . .

And moments of animal well-being
may be all that's left us, may well be.

To be grateful for neutral days.

To snip a strip of char
from a blackened wick, then watch
how the lamp comes alive again.

Then

There was a place of ruin
under the floor.
Familiar as your own hands.
Chaos had begun to gather there
like a murk in unused corners.
It was like winter dirt
between windowpanes – like
mould threading the bread.

Something sat on you
like a sandbag in those days.
Sat on your chest in the morning.

Sometimes even now the
huge and terrible face of
your past wrong turns around
to look at you
from its fixed distance.
And you see it is
still there, the terrible face,
it is not gone,
even when turned
the other way.

Where had you to go but
on from there?

Words became few, became poor, then
slowly began to
muscle back.

Gate

A pause to pull socks up.

It seems the time has come
to check your raggedy sadnesses
at the gate,
and take your place in line again
for the roulette of days.

Time to turn your back on
that other one, your nemesis,
a face that looks backward and weeps
while the feet walk blind
into the future;
time to drop hands with that one.

You have come into a place
of unbleached reckoning.
It is like
an empty dress,
wind filling an empty dress
hung out to air,
revolving slowly on its hanger,
catching the sun in its full
sleeves, in its folds and weave.

Hope, that shy fern,
has begun to unfurl its plume
from the rotted stump of your
cut down dream.

After the Storm

The leaf that under
the dripping eaves
receives
rain's overflow,
the darkened leaf, and shiny –
leaf at the end
of the thin branch straying
nearest the wall

has to bow sharply
under the impact
of each drip that falls,
and does so with the
crispness of a
Hasid praying.

II. Heat of the Immediate

Brink

Half moon still lit like a lamp
in a crack-of-dawn sky
greets my one open eye.
Mind skips like a stone
on the surface of waking;
thoughts that wing
out of dream, words unpinned
from their meanings
flurry the air like moths.

Shall I slip again
down the well of sleep,
sleep well?
What a blank ache
is day,
its labyrinthine paths.

I need soaring room.
I need roaring room.
The world gets in my way.

Once was full summer

Once was full summer.
Down the valley blew
a cheesecloth wind,
screening the curds of cloud
from the whey of haze.

Soon the mists burned off.
Sun sipped the dew
from the long grasses,
then laid them limp with heat;
waxing towards mid-day,
made them sweat
their own juices,
meadow-sweet.

Sun made his rounds
under the blue dome,
striding his realm
while all afternoon
hills cooled facing hills
with their shadows.

Lull

Drunken bees cling
and doze in the cups
of the rainy hollyhocks

and afternoon is still,
the day a dull silver.

Summer malingers.
Soon she will drop
her kid gloves
and abdicate to fall,

but for now
this lull
is our cradle.

To the Lookout

Will you remember that last fine
day of fall – how warm the
sun was, on our faces, how
cold the air – and shadows, speckling
the stone stairs, like water, moving?
Easily I go back there, following
our steps that were hasty, eager
to arrive. We could see for miles
that day, the leaves holding, in no
hurry to let go . . . we lay propped
on our elbows, side by side,
on the hill's crest, looking over –
the view so new – And still I hear,
like summer signing off, that faint
whirr in the grass:
crickets, or our bodies
talking to each other.

Echoes in November

Correspondences are everywhere,
things that shadow things,
that breathe or borrow
essence not their own;
and so the yellow leaves
that, singly, streak
in silence past a black
uncurtained pane
(catching the lamplight from within
as they dart down)
have the elusiveness
of shooting stars,
and so it sometimes happens
that you pause
in kitchen ministrations,
knife in hand
above the chopping board,
savouring, raw, a stub
of vegetable not destined
for the pot,
and faintly tasting
at the back of the palate
the ghost of a rose
in the core of the carrot.

Tenacious

A leaf. A brown leaf.
How a small brown leaf clings
to its twig, against the huge
whiteness of winter sky!
How it clings!

Munificent

O sky!
says the winter tree
with arms extended

(and sky bends low to
fill them with snow.)

Last of December

All over the city, white
musings of chimney smoke
unwind their chiffon into day,
wisps ribboned by wind
flicker, the sun's cold eye
recessed under lids of cloud
spindles its beam.
Christmas is done.
This is the great
lying-in, no one walks
abroad here, the snow lies
trackless in the empty streets.
No sound – not even a bird.
Curtains still drawn at noon.
Kettles are heating in every kitchen
for the birthing year.

Minus 20

Friends meet by chance
on a snowy street:
a winter kiss
bolstered by down,
and the clash of steamed lenses.
Dancing in place to keep warm,
we exchange pleasantries – snow
creaks underfoot as our
breaths mingle visible
in the air.

Flash

The heat of the immediate:
where is it now?
Was it our portion only for a spell,
like children's breath on windowpanes
in which to trace the day's
faces and names?
Damp breath exhaled on glass,
a cloud on which to skate
a stuttering finger –
quick, while it lasts –

Heat was a given, we thought.
Heat of connection.
Heat of breeding.
Our hot palms on the world.
Then a coolness set in.
When did it begin?

Heat of the immediate
is leaving me now,
surging up through the stem of me
in periodic gusts,
making me its conduit
to the world outside.
I who was warm in the world
and warmed by it
now do my part in warming it,
delivering my small
caloric quota to air's waiting arms,
in calibrated increments
that cool me as they go.

Cooled will I abide
in the world then,
till breath no longer clouds the mirror –

till one day, also briefly, my decay
will warm an inch or two
of the encompassing clay.

A Splinter

Under the nail of the right
pinky, clear to the cuticle.
Driven in like a spike.
A toothpick-sized wedge
of old wood, none too clean –
don't ask how it got in.
We're here today
to see how it gets out.

Among bleeders and breathers
through oxygen cones, among hobblers
on double canes, among the stretchers,
we are here with our splinter.
We are here with our right baby finger
extended aloft, held delicately up
and angled like a lady's to the handle
of her bone china cup.

Feeling a little fraudulent, oh more
than a little foolish, we are here
with our fiery-hot fingertip, red
as a pepper (whose taut shiny pad
feels like to burst open, to split
like a sausage casing and spit
out its meaty insides) – as we wait
for a doctor to rule on our splinter:

all told, full five hours of fidget
for the sake of a digit.
Then a ten-minute procedure.
The needle, the scalpel, the tourniquet,

tetanus top-up, a wipe-up of ooze,
a dressing of gauze; at last a prescription.
Day's redemption: to learn the infection
soon would have spread to the bone,

that we near lost a finger – caught in the nick! –
for a paltry rough sliver wedged under a nail.
– But that is just telling the tale.
A splinter, now what is a splinter?
A broken-off bit of the mass of what's Other,
come to invade, to pierce to the quick?
Something to bleed around – waken us – fret us?
So breath itself lodges in us.

In an Evening Window

She pares fruit
with a pearl handled knife.
The moon wants a fingernail
to fullness.
Nearly translucent are the thin
slices of pear
she raises to her lips,
traces of their nectar
like a fine dew
wetting her fingertips.

Out Like a Lion

It is another day of spring retreating
from its own premature and giddy feints
of a week gone. A few irregularly sized
mean flakes of snow, like white flies, circulate
among the multiple bare arms
of the window tree, seeming to dodge
the random stiff swingings in fickle wind.
Sky is a mix of glare and gloom
in various dismal whites. A limey wash
spills chill into the room.

It is another day of spring sprung back
upon itself, plea-bargaining against winter's
last stand. As for those sheathed,
red, shy-gleaming shoots that broke ground
this day or two past, in the raised bed
nestled against the house – best write them off.
These bully flakes circle and flex
and there is no mistaking their design,
which is to call reinforcements in, and loose
a last late blizzard down.

Blowing the Fluff Away

for E. B.

The sprig of unknown bloom you sent last fall
spent the long winter drying on my wall,
mounted on black. But it had turned to fluff
some months ago. Tonight I took it down
because I thought that I had had enough
of staring at it. Brittle, dry and brown,
it seemed to speak too plainly of a waste
of friendship, forced to flower, culled in haste.

So, after months of fearing to walk past
in case the stir should scatter it to bits,
I took it out to scatter it at last
with my own breath, and so to call us quits.
– Fooled! for the fluff was nothing but a sheath,
with tiny, perfect flowers underneath.

Mile End, April into June

i

Spring, oh sing
it has come,
sing it's here –
strange things are a-bloom
on Laurier Street.
See, someone has stuck
a child's pink mitten
(plucked from the sandy curb)
on the stick of a still-bare branch
of one of the city's potted saplings.
Gay it is in the sun,
saluting who comes;
around it new buds
have just begun to swell.

ii

Spring rain all night and
now a day of it, coming
in intermittent sudden patterings,
brief soaking showers, darkening
the bark of trees.
And in between,
blowing in through the winter-
rusted screen – purest of winds,
breath of a world
swept clean.

iii

What a glitter up and down the wire
as sudden sun strikes
yesterday's raindrops!

iv

Things that wash up
in winter's wake: an old sink
up-ended on a balcony,
seen through the open door –
flicker of maple leaves
in the drain hole,
the drain
draining air.

v

Next door, in the sunny hours
of the afternoon,
someone has put a parrot
on the balcony. It screams

an exotic scream, and at once
from the adjacent balcony
a child mimics it.

There is a silence then.
The parrot apparently
nonplussed by this
role reversal.

vi

Hot at last. On Avenue du Parc
old men in undershirts
lean out of upstairs windows,
elbows on the sill.
Mornings and evenings they lean out
from small dark rooms,
their faces striped
with sun and shadow.

vii

By the kitchen door, the cat
catches in his paw
the first fly of summer
and eats it, still buzzing.

III. The Briefest Room

Handful

Hands cupped round a butterfly
make a kind of filigree ball
of flesh and bone.
The lace they make
is owing to the space
between cracked fingers
spread to let in air
and form a peephole chamber
for the winged one
beating there.

Wilder vibration
soon tickles tender palms
into surprised alarm.
It is the briefest room:
walls fall away
to let the captive thing escape,
whose witnessed liberation
tickles the nape.

Lowly

Pink as discarded chewing gum
it comes to the surface in rain.
Segmented like a bellows.
Hoisting its length in sections
along puddled asphalt.
It is all muscle; elastic.
It draws itself forward in rhythms
of flex and slack.
It retracts when touched.

It is mute.
It abides in the dark, under porches.
It operates below ground
its tunnelings aerate.
It thrives on decay –
each day
casts many times its weight
in black gold,
giving back better than it takes.
It is the sign of living earth.

Hand picked, dropped in a tin can,
it is the fisherman's best friend.
It dwells in the smell
of good black loam
and the moisture thereof.
And it is moist, and gleams
in the loam like a tongue.

When caught, it writhes.
When cold, it goes deeper
underground and weaves itself
into a ball of its kind.
Slice it with a spade

and it seems
at least one part
survives,
burrowing back
into churned dirt.
Intact, it will die
when dry.
It shuns the sun.

Clock Song

(A Farewell to Hands, in a Digital Age)

Time creeps, time flies.
Clocks keep it and tell it,
tick it and tock it,
stand watch on a mantel
or hide in a pocket.
They have hands and faces,
but no eyes.
Clocks tell time.
(What do they tell it?)
They measure it out,
not to buy it or sell it
but just for good measure.
Some clocks chime.
Some loom in high places.
Some clocks hoard a treasure
of jewels in their works.
Clocks beat like hearts,
have stops and starts.
Their second hands move in tiny jerks.
Clocks need us to wind them
and keep them true.
We depend on clocks, too,
but don't always mind them.
A clock can wake us
or put us to sleep,
can lag or leap,
but *even a stopped clock*
is right twice a day —

so the wags say.
Clocks, clocks!
They do what they do.
Some sing Cuckoo.
Some say, "On your mark!"
Some glow in the dark.
And some stop for keeps
when an old man dies.
(Time creeps,
time flies.)

Detritus

Here is a bushel of strangers
strangely familiar: junked photos
and old letters, some still
in their envelopes, inks
of different hues,
long-ago stamps and postmarks,
snapshots with scalloped edges – each
a trace of a loved one
(somebody's, whose?)
a moment, a face,
smiling or un-,
or asquint in sun,
doted-on features bleached out
or blackened by shadow.
Throwaways, three deep.

A dusty barrel in a block-long
three-level parking garage
turned weekend flea market
of penny collectibles – this
dim-lit emporium, wandered into
on a bleak Saturday in December;
a barrel filled pell-mell with the
piecemeal leavings of lives
no one's left to remember –
here among the rows
of rickety tables bristling
with baubles, among leaning racks
crammed with threadbare velvet,
the lampshades, the vases,
the pervasive cellar smells,

is this cache of lost faces.
Ciphers for sale.
Pull them out by the fistful
and feel the dizziness, the
fitful pathos of years;
for a dollar or two
that one in your hand is yours.

In a Wink

What we call staring
isn't. Or not for long.
Reflex kicks in – the eye
on automatic wash
from the moment we waken.
What we call seeing
is no continuum
but a constant eclipsing,
sight given and taken,
chronic mini-blackouts
we sustain unaware.
Try to live without blinking
even a minute.
Only the dead stare.

Ho Hum

A yawn is guileless. It disarms.

And yet we early learn
the protocols of Yawn:
Cover your mouth.
Make like an Indian, *wah-wah-wah.*
Hide it, if you can.

A stifled yawn pops the ears,
spares others a sighting
of tonsils. Tongue curls
backwards in its cradle,
jaw winches its hinges,
eyes wink to slits and skin
draws tight around the mouth;

in the cave of the throat
a controlled wind
shudders and dies.

Gesundheit

Orgasm of the nose
the sneeze
builds to hair-trigger pitch
and sweet release.
Echoes itself, betimes.
Atchoo . . . aaaatchoo! (it rhymes),
or comes in multiple,
whole strings of sneeze.

Sneeze ladylike, in a hanky.
Sneeze workmanlike, in a grab
of the grubby shirt.
Or (caught unawares)
sneeze a grand unprotected sneeze
in open air.

Some with a toothpick or a twist
of tissue, tease a sneeze,
a private trick to clear the sinuses.
A sneeze rattles the face.
Loosens the mucus.
Paves the way for the trumpeting
honk and blow –

A pepper sneeze, a pollen sneeze,
a feather sneeze, all alike
pledge to untickle in a rush,
give leave to raise
a just-a-minute finger
before succumbing to the flush –
a microsecond's uncontrol,
a dispensation to go blotto
with impunity,

going where it takes us,
brakeless,
making the noisy noise
it makes us make.

A sneeze bobs the head.
Single or double bob,
or strings of pigeon bob,
brings blessings down on it.

View from the Treadmill

Where there are pigeons, there is
always an old man, or a man
one way or another hobbled
in his living, who has staked
out his spot among them, has
benched himself beside pigeons.
Like this one today,
come to the small *Terrasse*
we gaze down on, through this wall
of glass – to take his share of the
day and air, even in winter:

Dark toque drawn down
to his eyebrows, open overcoat,
neck scarf wound round and round
and pant legs bunched above big boots,
he has no bag of bread
for the piebald birds; that's
not his game. (Now and again they
all fly up, flashing the white
of underwings – then all
come down again, not far away.)
He occupies his space – talks
to his cigarette, the air,
the pigeons – talks with his hands
(ungloved and oddly graceful)
with jabbing gestures
and sudden outflung fingers
– or reaches down between his feet
for the familiar bottle cloaked
in its paper bag, lifts it to lips
for a skyward tilt.

This too is a life.
Who is to say that it is
worse than yours or mine?
More reprehensible? We anyway
all come to the same end.
He has his pleasures, has
his flock, that mill and bob
at his feet . . . the sky today
is marbled, all a mass
of mottled cloud like clotted cream
lit smoky gold by a dim
gleam-through of December sun,
and it is at his fingertips.

Reminder

Out of station darkness wends
the early morning train
on tracks that abut mean streets.
Why do windows of slums flash
like jewels in the sunrise
as we pass them by?

To the power of *n*

Anything dwelt-on to excess
turns otherly –
sound of a word, a name,
shape of a hand or foot,
look of a face – even one's own
in a mirror, stared at overly.
(Known becomes strange becomes dumb.)
Children soon guess
how easily the world
can be undone;
how we can repeat a thing
into oblivion.

Poem on Father's Day

There appears suddenly, out of nowhere,
a blemish in the mirror
on a piece of sentimental furniture,
a bubble in the bevel
of the scalloped border.

Where are you now, my father,
fifty-four years gone,
whose adolescent face once looked
back at itself from this mirror?
(Father it wasn't given me to know.
Father I never called on Father's Day.)

Truth burns through a dream.
Sometimes I have felt
your presence in a dream,
have dreamed about you.
Today, thinking of you,
I dialed your brother, last
of the living uncles.

But how am I to read
this pucker in the silver?
A flaw, shaped like a tear.
Last time I looked, it wasn't there.

It is your mother's face
that looks back at me now
from the glass – she who outlived you
forty-eight years – but not the wizened face
I said goodbye to; it is her face

as you last knew it, face I remember
from when I was small,
I see framed here.

The son I named for you
turns thirty this week.

Somewhere at the back of my mind
an old clock goes on chiming the quarters,
a clock of my childhood.

Parents

It is in the nature
of a mother
to hover.
All mothering
is at least one part
hovering.
What would you rather?
Angels in heaven
also hover – sometimes fall.
We all have the mothers
we were given. And
breakable fathers.

Are you serious?

What is that little grating chink
in college girls' voices, like the chirp
of glass marbles rubbed together
in a child's palm?
It is some kind of hope
they are grinding in their throats,
a virus they catch from one another.
It is like birds that cock their heads
at the foot of picnic tables.
They think it will fetch them something.

Run With It

The road through the park
is littered with sticks
discarded by dogs
on their morning walks.
Sticks don't go home with dogs.
Dropped by the wayside
they lie in wait,
like the theories of philosophers.

Messenger

Little stone in my shoe,
what have you to tell me?
That such a tiny irritant can serve
to undermine a meditative mood
hard-won from day's commotion
by a walker on the mountain?
That I am obstinate, who will not stoop,
or stop to teeter on one leg
and tug at sandal straps –
prefer to hope you'll work your way
out, same way you sidled in,
without my intervention?

Are you a stowaway – fugitive,
or just adventurer
hopping a ride to town,
a roadside pebble with big city dreams?
Are you a terrorist – dispatched
to tell the plight of kindred
tired of being trodden on?
Are you a grain of sand,
seed for a pearl to my oyster brain?
Are you an augurer?

You cling and dig in
even to toughened skin,
and will not be appeased.
Little stone in my shoe,
what makes me choose
to walk with you awhile?
What little creeping guilt
accepts it as my lot
that you should harry my sole
the whole way home?

Getting On

Ailments and aches assail us after fifty,
Each our own. Familiar they become,
Demanding succour, vying for our time
As once our children did. It isn't nifty.
The pills and unguents cost a pretty penny.
Our calendar fills up with consultations.
Maintenance of the body taps a patience
In short supply – if ever we had any.

Once we could drift, but now we have to row.
Merrily down the stream? It seems not so.
What kind of boat is this? What kind of pond?
We're bailing madly, but the truth is stark:
A one-way ticket to the Great Beyond
Is issued each of us when we embark.

Seen from a Moving Train

"so much depends/ upon . . ."

A derelict auto hull
in a spring-green pasture:
festive with rust
under the rain

– Lucky am I in my still
nimble brain, its
trustiness.

The Well

A well of the sweetest water
was ours, unsought; we drew,
and we did drink.
But time went by –
we did not think
to dig it deeper, dig it new.
Our well is dry.

How shall we dig it deeper
now, with these aging hands?
We must not ask.
Strength will be given.
Turn to the task,
find in it heart to understand
what thirst has driven.

Pause for Breath

We are not digging very well.
We have flagged in the digging.

– Digging for water, for treasure?
To China? Or digging our own graves?

Perhaps they're all the same.
Perhaps it doesn't matter.

It's the digging that saves.

A Snow Fence

Bodiless God Who art wind,
what are these little miseries?

Pity our walking bones,
their worn ball bearings.

The ink is clotted in the pen,
and the thoughts in the chill brain.

Can we have come so soon
to the end of our chalk?

Lo, I went out into the afternoon.
A snow fence wavered dark red

up hill, down dale, against drifts
like dunes, under a sky like smoke.

It was very still.
So quiet was the quiet

I could hear snowflakes
kissing my hat.

I stood, and listened for an answer.
Felt my heart beat.

Span

We write on Time
until our rhyme
runs out,
until the chalk itself
has dwindled to a nub
and less than that,
a smudge of powder
on a fingertip,
a powder shed
upon the ground.

Our frail agency
in the world, this:
our brave chalk line,
our mark on Time –
first firm, then skipping
like a vapour trail,
and soon enough rubbed out
by Time's felt brush
in Time's fell hand
(or by a celestial Thumb.)

What then can our intrepid cursive prove?
– Still, let us make our rhyme a rhyme of love.

Peaks

i

Gaining zenith, its till-
now hidden prospect, still
we lose a long view:
something to climb to.
Once over the ridge, what's left
but the descent?
Now we have seen
what there was to see.
Our lodestone gone,
journey's next leg
a comedown, either way
we play it: backtrack
or soldier on.

ii

How we have lost, lost, lost –
And how we lose
from the moment we yield ourselves,
face in each other's eyes –
as every summit takes back promise
and surprise,
and solstice in the swoon of June
is but a turning to the dark again.

But oh, the lovely risk!
The lovely risk love is.

Brush

Always a wild openness
to the left and right of our path,
a humming in the high grasses.
What is it holds us to our course?

A pagan recklessness in my past
makes me conservative.

Today when I was reading on the balcony
a bee buzzed my knuckle, close enough
for me to feel the wind of his wings,

and all day long I have gone on feeling
the wind of those wings.

Acknowledgements

My thanks to the editors of the following journals in which these poems first appeared:

The Antigonish Review: 'To the power of *n*'

Arc: 'Echoes in November', 'A Snow Fence'

Canadian Notes & Queries (web exclusive): 'The Well', 'Brush', *'Are you serious?'*

Carousel: 'Out Like a Lion'

CV2: 'Tenacious', 'Munificent', 'Last of December', 'Minus 20', 'Brink', 'Once was full summer', 'After the Storm'

Event: 'Mile End, April into June'

The Fiddlehead: 'Pent', 'In the Middle of the Night', 'A Splinter', 'Dry Spring', 'Gate', 'Detritus', 'Messenger'

The Hudson Review: 'Clock Song', 'Handful', 'Peaks', 'In an Evening Window', 'Pause for Breath'

Jewish Quarterly: 'A Prayer for Prayer'

Literary Review of Canada: 'Breakfast and Morning Paper'

Maisonneuve: 'Gesundheit'

The New Quarterly: 'Then', 'Span', 'The Star', 'Flash', 'Parents'

North American Review: 'Lull'

Nth Position (online): 'Wake'

Ploughshares: 'Poem on Father's Day'

PN Review: 'Song', 'Screens'

Poetry: 'Blowing the Fluff Away'

The Threepenny Review: 'Lowly', 'In a Wink'

The Walrus: 'As a storm-lopped tree'

I am grateful to the Conseil des arts et des lettres du Québec and to the Canada Council for the Arts for their support at different stages in the completion of this body of work.

Special thanks to my first readers: Bruce Taylor, Don Coles, and Eric Ormsby.

About the Author

Robyn Sarah was born in New York City to Canadian parents, and has lived for most of her life in Montreal. Her poetry began appearing in Canadian literary magazines in the early 1970s, while she completed studies in philosophy at McGill University and music at the Conservatoire du Québec. In 1976, with Fred Louder, she co-founded Villeneuve Publications and co-edited its poetry chapbook series which included first titles by August Kleinzahler, A. F. Moritz, and others. The press folded in 1987. During the same years and until 1996, she taught English at Champlain Regional College. The author of several poetry collections, two collections of short stories, and a collection of essays on poetry, she has published widely in Canadian and American journals. Her poems have been anthologized in *Fifteen Canadian Poets x 3, The Bedford Introduction to Literature, The Norton Anthology of Poetry,* and in Garrison Keillor's *Good Poems for Hard Times.*